Crazy for Puppies!

Jo Ellen Bogart

Photography
Mark Raycroft

Scholastic Canada Ltd.
Toronto New York London Auckland Sydney
Mexico City New Delhi Hong Kong Buenos Aires

Scholastic Canada Ltd.
604 King Street West, Toronto, Ontario M5V 1E1, Canada

Scholastic Inc.
557 Broadway, New York, NY 10012, USA

Scholastic Australia Pty Limited
PO Box 579, Gosford, NSW 2250, Australia

Scholastic New Zealand Limited
Private Bag 94407, Greenmount, Auckland, New Zealand

Scholastic Children's Books
Euston House, 24 Eversholt Street
London, NW1 1DB, UK

Photo credits:
All photos © Mark Raycroft, with the following exceptions:
Page 8 Poodle © Photographs Barbara Augello
Page 9 Poodle © Close Encounters of the Furry Kind
Page 20 Shih Tzu © rr4pictures
Page 35 Labradoodle © Libby Chapman

Library and Archives Canada Cataloguing in Publication
Bogart, Jo Ellen, 1945-
Crazy for puppies / Jo Ellen Bogart.

ISBN 0-439-94915-7
1. Dogs--Pictorial works--Juvenile literature.

I. Title.
SF430.B64 2006   j636.7'07'0222   C2005-906894-9

ISBN-10 0-439-94915-7 / ISBN-13 978-0-439-94915-6
Text copyright © 2006 by Jo Ellen Bogart.
All rights reserved.

6 5 4 3 2   Printed in Singapore   07 08 09 10

Table of Contents

Labrador Retriever

Even as a pup, this Labrador Retriever is a sturdy little guy. He has strong, straight legs and big paws. He loves to play games and spend time with his people. It will take years for him to lose his puppy playfulness, but he will grow up to be a well-rounded dog and a loyal friend.

Labrador Retrievers originated as fishermen's helpers in Newfoundland. They were trained to haul fishing nets out of the water. In the 1800s some Labs were brought to Britain where they were trained to retrieve game. The Lab is still popular there, but British Labs are heavier and thicker than their North American cousins.

Labrador Retrievers love the water, and were bred to be great swimmers. They grow up to have dense, hard coats that shed water and protect them from low branches and brush. Underneath their hard coats are soft undercoats that keep them warm in cold water. These wonderful coats are often black, but many Labs are yellow, and a few are chocolate brown. All three colours of Labs can be born into the same litter. The Lab tail, broader at the base and tapering towards the tip, acts as a rudder when the dog swims. This is called an "otter" tail. Labs even have webbing between their toes!

Labrador Retrievers are highly intelligent and very trainable. They have a real devotion to work and are adaptable to many situations. Because of this, they perform admirably in many areas of service, especially as guide dogs for the blind.

Labs are also extremely good-natured and easygoing. Even their eyes seem to smile. They make fine family pets: friendly to all and great with children.

Height: 53–61 centimetres
Weight: 25–36.2 kilograms

2

Golden Retriever

Do these puppies look a bit like Labrador Retrievers to you? If you look closely, you'll see that they have longer, wavier hair. This means that these roly-poly puppies are actually Golden Retrievers. They are very intelligent, friendly and playful. With the right handling, they will grow up to be gentle companions that are good with other animals and children.

The Golden Retriever got its start in England during the mid-1800s, when Lord Tweedmouth bred his yellow retriever with a Tweed Water Spaniel. Later, other breeds were mixed in, including the Irish Setter and probably the Bloodhound.

The Golden first appeared in North America in the 1920s. Since then it has become very popular, both because of its hunting talents, and because it makes such an exceptional family pet and friend. Because Golden Retrievers are so popular, it is important to find a breeder who takes great care in choosing the parents for a litter.

The Golden Retriever's coat ranges from a rich, deep golden colour to a light creamy gold. As with all water dogs, the Golden has an outer coat that is dense and water-repellent, plus a warm, soft undercoat. When they are full-grown, these Golden pups will have lovely ruffs on their necks and feathering along their legs. These coats will need some brushing to keep them neat and untangled.

This breed, as with the Labrador Retriever, can get a bit chubby, so owners need to make sure that their Golden Retrievers receive the right amounts of food and exercise. Romping in the park, chasing a ball, running in a field or swimming will make these pooches happy. To keep them out of mischief, they will need their minds challenged as well.

The trustworthy Golden is known for its fine temperament, as well as for its athletic skills and trainability. This breed will bark at strangers, but it does not have a strong guarding instinct. Kind-hearted Goldens also make fine guide dogs or therapy dogs. Some people might fault them for their occasional over-exuberance and need for human companionship, but most Golden Retriever lovers find that's just part of their charm.

Height: 54–61 centimetres
Weight: 25–34 kilograms

German Shepherd Dog

When we see a German Shepherd pup frolicking with her littermates, it can be hard to imagine what serious jobs she might hold once she's grown. The highly intelligent and trainable German Shepherd Dog has long been used as a police dog, a guard dog and a guide dog. You can also find this breed working as rescue dogs, bomb squad dogs and detector dogs, often called sniffer dogs.

German Shepherds were bred from herding dogs in Bavaria, Germany in the 1800s. The first German Shepherd was registered in 1899 by German Captain Max von Stephanitz. Europe was becoming more industrialized, and von Stephanitz wanted to develop an intelligent breed of dogs who could adapt to the changing times and be useful in many situations.

The German Shepherd has a double coat for protection and warmth. Most of the dogs have the well-known tan shorthair coat with black markings. Show dogs can also be black and grey, or solid black. Sometimes German Shepherds can be found with longer hair and in other colours like cream, white or sable. Some kennel clubs recognize the White Shepherd as a separate breed.

German Shepherds are very protective of their homes and their families. They are alert, eager to serve and almost fearless. There is hardly a doggy skill that this breed does not possess. Pups should be well socialized to prevent overly aggressive behaviour, and a breeder should be chosen with care. This energetic breed is happiest when it has lots of exercise and challenging activities.

Famous German Shepherd Dog:
A German Shepherd Dog, rescued from a German dog kennel and trained by U.S. Corporal Lee Duncan in World War I, became a movie and TV star known the world over. The dog's name was Rin Tin Tin.

Height: 56–66 centimetres
Weight: 35–40 kilograms

Poodle

Some people believe that Poodles are just fancy dogs with unusual haircuts. But Poodles are very clever and athletic dogs. They are among the most intelligent of dog breeds. With their strength and nimbleness, they also excel in obedience and agility exercises.

While Poodles have always been valued as retrievers, they have also been very successful street and circus performers.

Although some people link Poodles to France, the breed began in Germany. The Poodle was known in Europe by the 15th century and was featured in paintings of the time. It was very popular in France during the reign of King Louis XIV and is still sometimes referred to as the French Poodle.

There are three sizes of poodles (Miniature, Toy and Standard) but they are classified as one breed. The smaller types of poodle were bred down from the Standard poodle.

The fluffy, non-shedding coat of the Poodle is always growing and requires regular clipping. Show Poodles must be clipped in one of four accepted styles: the Lion trim, also called the English Saddle; the Continental; the Sporting or Lamb trim and the Puppy clip. The last is permitted only for show dogs less than one year of age. These clips often involve shaved areas of skin next to bunches of hair. The reason for these clips can be traced back to the Poodle's history as a water retriever. The clipped sections, usually on the legs, make swimming easier. The remaining hair keeps important body parts warm in the cold water.

If left uncut, Poodles' coats can also be formed into a corded style of long twisted lengths. Poodles come in colours such as apricot, cream, grey, blue, black, white, brown, café au lait and silver. Poodles of more than one colour are not accepted at many shows.

Poodles have an air of dignity, but at the same time they can be playful, cheerful and very bright.

Did you know that the name Poodle comes from the German word *pudeln*, which means to do the dog paddle, or to splash in water?

Height: Toy, up to 25.4 centimetres; Miniature, 25.4–38.1 centimetres; Standard, 38.1 centimetres and up
Weight: (approximate):
Toy, 3–4 kilograms;
Miniature, 7–8 kilograms;
Standard, 20–32 kilograms

Shetland Sheepdog

These adorable pups may look like miniature Collies, but they aren't the same breed at all. Even when grown, Shetland Sheepdogs are only knee high. They may look pretty and delicate, but Shelties are sturdy dogs with a strong will to work.

Shetland Sheepdogs originated in the Shetland Islands, off the coast of Scotland. They were bred from a variety of dogs that visited from the ships that docked there. Sheltie ancestors might have included Spitz type dogs (northern breeds of dogs with tails that curl upwards) from Scandinavia, Greenland Yakki dogs and King Charles Spaniels.

Over time Shelties developed a protective double coat, suitable for the weather of the Shetland Islands. Strong muscles and a sure step allowed them to get around on the rugged countryside. They skilfully guided and protected the small Shetland Island sheep, cattle and ponies. They also kept livestock out of farmers' vegetable gardens. It's not hard to see why Shelties are winners in today's obedience and agility competitions.

The long, luxurious coat of the Sheltie can be sable, black, tri-colour or merle (bluish-grey streaked with black). It needs to be brushed every week to help reduce shedding.

The coat is never trimmed, but the hair between the dog's toe pads must be kept tidy.

Shelties make good family pets. They are loyal to and affectionate with all members of their families. As with many herding dogs, they can be a bit aloof with strangers. Owners should socialize their dogs at an early age by letting them meet lots of nice, friendly people.

Shelties have been known to herd children, even nipping at their heels as if they were sheep. These dogs also like to keep an eye on their people to make sure they are safe. Many Shelties might bark a bit more than their owners would like, but that's what makes them such great watch dogs!

Did you know that Shelties were also called Toonies, after a Norwegian word for a small piece of land? Because of their size, they've also been called Peerie (fairy) dogs.

Height: 33–41 centimetres
Weight: 5-8 kilograms

Miniature Schnauzer

Miniature Schnauzer pups come into the world as tiny black bundles of fur. While some pups remain black as they grow up, others begin to turn salt and pepper (black and grey), just like the pups in these pictures. The small dogs may look delicate, but they are actually very sturdy and well muscled.

The Miniature Schnauzer is a good-natured dog that gets along well with children. It is affectionate, but not in a sloppy, overly excited way. It's intelligent, and though it can be stubborn at times, it does well in obedience training.

Schnauzers come in three sizes: Miniature, Standard and Giant. Unlike Poodles, the three sizes are considered to be different breeds because they have different kinds of ancestors. The Miniature is included in the Terrier group, but the Giant and Standard Schnauzers are classified as working dogs. A German breeding program developed the Miniature Schnauzer from the Standard Schnauzer and other dogs, such as the Affenpinscher. It may also have the Poodle in its lineage. The Giant Schnauzer was developed for herding by crossing the Standard Schnauzer with larger breeds of dogs.

The Miniature Schnauzer's coat requires quite a bit of care. The top layer of its double coat is wiry and hard, but the short undercoat is soft. Show dogs have their coats stripped, or plucked, by hand. Pet dogs can be clipped, which is easier and less expensive, yet still attractive. The Schnauzer has a beard, a moustache and eyebrows, all called furnishings. These are kept long and require lots of care. The ones around the mouth can get especially messy. Schnauzers' ears can be clipped and trained to stand up, or left natural and bent over. Tails are usually docked (cut short) before the pups' eyes open.

The Miniature Schnauzer can be counted on to bark at strangers, but will not act as a guard dog. This breed might need to be encouraged to reduce the volume and length of a barking session — it likes to let you know how it's feeling!

Did you know that the word Schnauzer is from the German word for snout or muzzle?

Height: 30–36 centimetres
Weight: 5–7 kilograms

Yorkshire Terrier

This elf-like Yorkshire Terrier pup will grow up to be a small dog with a floor-skimming coat of tan in front and steel blue in back. His little face will be framed by pointy ears and, often, a bow tied in a topknot of hair. His tail will be docked, and its hair will be kept long to join his skirt of fur. However, if he is not a show dog, his owner might choose to keep his coat short, casual and fluffy.

The Yorkshire Terrier's ancestors are thought to include the Waterside Terrier and other terriers from Scotland. These terriers travelled with the Scottish weavers who migrated to Yorkshire, England in the mid-1800s. The dogs, larger then, hunted rats in the wool mills. The weavers' dogs soon interbred with local dogs, and by 1865 the breed had become smaller and more similar to what we see today. In 1870 it appeared in the Westmoreland dog show and was given the name of Yorkshire Terrier.

Yorkshire Terriers are bundles of energy. Their adventurous ways and lively spirit are part of their toy Terrier breeding. They are quite active indoors, so they do not require a lot of outdoor exercise. Because Yorkies don't seem to realize how small they are, they must sometimes be protected from their boldness with other dogs.

They are suspicious enough of strangers to be good watchdogs. However, they are loyal and affectionate with their own people. Yorkies are fairly delicate and need careful handling to avoid injury. Some owners find the Yorkie difficult to housetrain and a bit barky, but these problems can usually be solved with good training. Owners should keep the Yorkie's ratting background in mind and not trust this little Terrier with small animals.

As with many small breeds, the Yorkshire Terrier can hope to enjoy a long life, with an average lifespan of 12–15 years.

Famous Yorkie: A Yorkie named Smoky, found in a jungle, became an army mascot in the South Pacific during WWII. She entertained troops with her tricks, flew on missions and visited the injured. She even performed a vital task: pulling a communications wire through a narrow pipe. She returned to the U.S. with her owner to a hero's welcome. She even had her own TV show!

Height: 15–17.5 centimetres
Weight: 3–4 kilograms

Beagle

This cute little pup is a Beagle. When he grows up, he will have a fine, baying voice and a fantastic sense of smell. His sturdy build makes him a great playmate for kids. He has a good appetite and is a delightfully unfinicky eater. All of this, along with an easy-to-groom coat, makes him a fine family pet.

Beagle-type dogs were known in Britain, Italy, France and Greece by the 14th century. They were used, usually in packs, for hunting rabbits and game birds. Probably bred down from Foxhounds, Beagles now come in two sizes: those less than 33 centimetres and those between 33 and 41 centimetres. At one time, some Beagles were small enough to fit into a hunter's saddlebag!

The Beagle often sports a coat with a tan head and a black saddle over a tan back. Its paws, chest, muzzle and tail tip are bright white. The white-tipped tail is held high so a hunter can easily follow it on the hunt. The Beagle's short coat does shed, so it will benefit from brushing to remove loose hairs.

When a hunting Beagle picks up the right scent, he uses his loud baying voice and "gives tongue" to announce the news. As a scent hound, he has a particularly strong sense of smell. His long ears drag the ground as he follows a trail and they help direct the scent to his nose. The wet surface of his nose holds scent particles. Sniffing helps stir up these particles so they can enter his long snout, which is filled with 200 million scent receptors.

These energetic hounds need lots of exercise. They also like to sniff around and might follow their noses off on an adventure. A good scent will make them ignore commands completely. Because of this, they should be kept on leashes and be allowed to play off leash only in fenced areas.

As pack dogs, Beagles love company and get along well with people and other dogs. Although their baying can sometimes be a problem, their winning personalities have made this breed extremely popular.

Famous Beagle: Snoopy, from Charles Schulz's *Peanuts* comics, is a beagle.

Height: from less than 33 centimetres to 33–41 centimetres
Weight: 9-11 kilograms

Bichon Frise

With its white cottony coat and jolly spirit, the Bichon Frise is a sweetheart of a dog. It is exceptionally good-natured and affectionate, as well as intelligent and easily trainable.

Bichon dogs are likely descended from the small white dogs that were popular in Mediterranean regions around 300 BC. These little dogs travelled with sailors and interbred with local dogs at any number of seaports. The Bichon Tenerife or, as we know it, the Bichon Frise, was developed on the island of Tenerife in the Canary Islands.

This sociable dog has been bred for centuries to be the perfect companion. It has often been the pampered pet of royalty and the wealthy. Over the years, many Bichons were even included in portraits with their masters.

In the late 1800s the Bichon Frise fell out of favour with the rich, and it became known as a talented street entertainer and circus dog. The breed began to be noticed again around 1930 in France.

It arrived in North America in the 1950s and was given official status as a breed here in 1973. Since then, its popularity has risen steadily.

The Bichon Frise's velvety and resilient double coat is usually given a rounded-off trim — it looks just like a powder puff!

Its coat does not shed, so it can be a good pet for people with allergies.

Because they're such people dogs, Bichon Frises make great additions to loving families.

Did you know that the name Bichon might have come from *barbichon*, the French word for goatee, a pointed little beard? Bichon Frise is short for *Bichon à poil frisé*, or Bichon of the curly coat.

Height: 23–30 centimetres
Weight: 3–5 kilograms

Shih Tzu

This tiny fluff-ball may look like a toy, but she will grow up to carry herself like a princess. Her head will be held high, her tail curled over her back. Perhaps this is because of her impressive ancestors. Shih Tzus can be traced to Tibet, where they were revered as sacred temple dogs.

In the 17th Century, Shih Tzus were taken from Tibet to China. They became much-treasured gifts to royalty and favourites of the Emperor. The Empress had a breeding kennel, and there the Tibetan dogs might have been interbred with Pugs and Pekingese to reduce their size. The breed came to North America in the late 1930s. At first it was a rare breed, but its popularity increased quickly, and more dogs were bred. Today the Shih Tzu is a much sought-after dog.

With such a regal carriage, Shih Tzus may seem aloof, but they are very affectionate pets. They seek and appreciate the attention of their owners, but they are friendly with strangers as well. Shih Tzus were always bred as companions, and they play this role very well. They are great family dogs, as they are not as fragile as some toy dogs.

This little dog grows an impressive double coat that is long and mainly straight or slightly wavy. The colour may be all black, grey and white, black and white, gold and white or all gold. A white tail tip is prized, as is a blaze up the dog's face. The hair on the bridge of its nose grows upwards and is usually tied up to allow the dog to see clearly. Long ears with long hair blend in with the rest of the coat. Daily grooming is required to avoid tangles and mats.

Some people choose to keep their pet Shih Tzus' coats short, so much less grooming is necessary. The dog will still need attention paid to its nails, eyes and ears. Shih Tzus have unusually long eyelashes and prominent eyes that are susceptible to irritation. The area around the eyes should be washed often, and eye drops may be required. Tzus also have crowded teeth that should be brushed regularly. This will keep them happy and healthy.

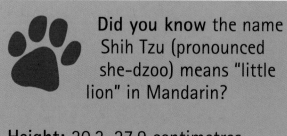

Did you know the name Shih Tzu (pronounced she-dzoo) means "little lion" in Mandarin?

Height: 20.3–27.9 centimetres
Weight: 4–7 kilograms

Boxer

What could be cuter than these big eyes, floppy ears and smushed-in noses? The Boxer face, with its wrinkles and forward facing eyes, is very expressive of the dog's mood, which is often jolly. These pups will be playful friends for years. They will grow strong muscles to help them bound after balls and make amazing leaps into the air.

In moments of sheer happiness, they will bend themselves into a kidney bean shape, their back ends wiggling in joy. In fact, Boxers can even make a "woo woo" sound when they are happy and excited. These pooches are highly recommended as family pets, though they need lots of socialization in their first months.

It might surprise you to find out that today's Boxers are descendants of fighting dogs from Tibet and boar hunting dogs from Belgium. These dogs demonstrated strength and stamina, as well as courage. To get the Boxer we know today, breeders also mixed in some Bulldog and Terrier.

Today's Boxer is a boisterous and friendly dog. It welcomes the chance to run and play and does well in sporting activities. These high-energy dogs need to be trained, especially to keep them from jumping up on people.

The Boxer's sleek coat can be kept neat by using a rubber brush to remove loose hairs. Colours for the coat include a tan colour, generally called fawn, and a pattern called brindle that mixes tan with speckled black stripes. The face is often black, and white markings on the chest and neck add a nice touch. The Boxer tail is usually docked and the ears, once cropped and trained to a point, now are usually left to hang down.

Their short coats don't give much warmth, so Boxers should not be left outside in the cold. They should also be watched in hot weather, because their short noses make it hard for them to breathe. It's important to take good care of Boxers in all sorts of weather to keep them healthy.

Did you know that the Boxer uses its front paws to "box," or paw the air, when playing?

Height: 53–63 centimetres
Weight: 24–32 kilograms

Bernese Mountain Dog

Look at this beautiful, smiling puppy. She's going to be a big one. Her handsome coat is mainly black, with rust-coloured cheeks and eyebrows, and a white blaze down her face and chest. White paws and tail tip finish off her striking markings. She has lots of Swiss Mountain Dog cousins with similar markings, but her breed is the only one with a long coat. This heavy coat makes her suited to cooler climates. Her coat will need regular brushing when it comes in

fully, but she should get used to being groomed while she is young.

Bernese Mountain Dogs are probably descended from the large mastiff-type dogs that were brought to Switzerland by the Romans 2,000 years ago. They remained there as farm dogs and were used for livestock herding and cart pulling. The breed came close to disappearing in the late 1800s, but was re-established by breeding the few dogs that were left on local farms. This tight inbreeding might have caused Bernese Mountain Dogs' health problems.

The Bernese Mountain Dog is intelligent, loyal and good-natured. It will not be a guard dog, but it makes a good watchdog. It needs obedience training with a gentle approach, since it is a sensitive dog.

Berners mature slowly, and the pups stay boisterous for a while. They also tend to be shy, so they should be socialized well.

The Berner is a fine companion breed with a good temperament. Its large size and wagging tail makes it the perfect dog for a family that will appreciate its enthusiasm.

Did you know that these dogs are sometimes called Berners, which is short for their Swiss breed name, Berner Sennenhunds? This name comes from the Swiss canton of Bern, where the dogs originated.
Height: 58–71 centimetres
Weight: 36–50 kilograms

Pomeranian

This perky little Pomeranian pup has some big ancestors. As a Spitz-type dog, he can claim cousins such as the Malamute, the Eskimo Dog, the Samoyed and the Husky. All of these dogs have what they need for cold climates: fine double coats to keep them warm, small ears that lie protected within their fur and long snouts to warm the air before it is breathed. This Pom pup has all of these in a smaller package.

Pomeranians weren't always this small. At one time they were about 16 kilograms and made good sheep-herding dogs. Today the breed usually weighs between 1.4 and 3 kilograms and is the smallest of the northern breeds. Despite its size, it retains its hunting instincts and spirited nature. It is a friendly and loyal pet. It is also a good little watchdog, though some might find it barks a little too much.

Poms are descended from the Northern Spitz dogs that were carried by sea traders to Pomerania. The breed became popular in England when Queen Victoria bought one named Marco in Italy. At that time most Poms were still a whopping 9 kilograms. The Queen encouraged the breeding of smaller dogs.

The first Poms were usually white or parti-coloured, which is white and another colour. In the process of reducing the Pomeranian's size, breeders introduced new colours and a thicker coat. The Pom's double coat, with its lion-like mane, is now seen in a dozen beautiful colours. One of the most popular is a bright orange. The Pomeranian's tiny face has a charming foxy look to it.

When these dogs were bred to be smaller, their teeth became crowded, so Pomeranian owners need to get out the toothbrush and get busy. With good care and a little luck, the Pomeranian puppy can expect to live well into its teens.

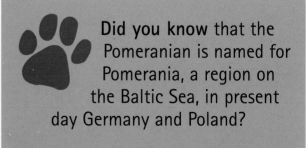

Did you know that the Pomeranian is named for Pomerania, a region on the Baltic Sea, in present day Germany and Poland?

Height: 18–23 centimetres
Weight: 1.4–3 kilograms

Soft-Coated Wheaten Terrier

Soft-Coated Wheaten Terrier pups are lovely dark bundles of fluff. They can be chocolate or light reddish brown, and some of these sturdy little guys have black masks. It will be more than a year before they grow the wheaten coat that gives the breed its name. This continuously growing, single coat will need frequent combing and regular trimming from the time a puppy is five months old.

The usual trim for the Soft-Coated Wheaten leaves long hair between the eyes and down through the face. The long hair on the muzzle, which looks a little like a beard, is sometimes bluish grey. The Wheaten's non-shedding coat makes the breed a good choice for people who are sensitive to dog hair.

The Soft-Coated Wheaten Terrier originated in Ireland around the 1700s. At that time the law did not allow peasants to own hunting dogs, so they designed their own versatile working dogs. They bred their dogs from stock such as the Kerry Blue and other Irish Terriers. The Wheaten served as a hunting dog, a herder, a watchdog and a ratter. As such, it was developed more for work than any particular look, and it became a capable, quick-witted dog.

For a Terrier, the Soft-Coated Wheaten is rather laid back. It is bouncy and alert, friendly and happy. It barks, but less than most Terriers. The Wheaten does show some of the well-known Terrier stubbornness, but obedience training should help. Its average intelligence and sensitive nature respond well to praise and rewards. While the Wheaten is a pretty peaceful dog, there might be minor battles with cats and between male dogs. As with all dogs, it's best to get them used to their people at an early age.

Height: 43–48 centimetres
Weight: 13.6–18.1 kilograms

Border Collie

In a wriggling litter of Border Collie pups, we might see coats of black and white, red and white, tri-colour, solid black, and merle. As the pups grow their coats, they might have long or short hair. Border Collies are bred more for brains and skill than for any particular colour or form. They excel at agility and obedience, and when we look at the list of smartest dogs, this amazing and interesting breed is at the top.

The Border Collie originated in the borderlands between England and Scotland, but has spread to many countries. Hundreds of generations of Border Collies have been bred for the specific job of herding, and they are extremely good at it. They control livestock with a stalking movement called the "moving crouch" and an intense stare called "eye." The Border Collie's ability to herd comes from its natural instinct to chase prey. Young Border Collies are tested for herding ability, then trained with small flocks of ducks. Border Collies often win the top prizes at herding competitions.

As well as brains, the Border Collie has a fine body with amazing stamina. It thrives on mental and physical activity. For a pet dog, the urge to work can often be satisfied with games, agility exercises and competition. Dogs that do not get enough activity can suffer from boredom, and that can lead to mischief and even nippiness. Socializing the dog as a pup helps lessen the natural shyness or aloofness that Border Collies share with other herding dogs.

Border Collies try to herd everything, from people to cars, but this tendency can be worked on with good training. You shouldn't run from a herding dog — you'll seem even more like a sheep in need of herding!

The loyal and faithful Border Collie is a wonderful pet for people who will spend the time to appreciate the breed's intelligence and talents.

Did you know that the border the name refers to is the land that lies between England and Scotland where Border Collies began? Or that Collie might come from a Celtic word for useful?

Height: 46–56 centimetres
Weight: 13.5–22 kilograms

Chihuahua

Chihuahuas are the world's smallest dogs, so you can just imagine how tiny their puppies are! They are very small and fragile. You could easily hold one in your hands.

A Chihuahua litter can have pups with long coats and pups with short coats. The pups might be different colours, and they might grow up to be slightly different sizes.

Most Chihuahua pups are born with a soft spot on their heads called a molera. It usually shrinks as they grow. For the first six months of a pup's life its ears are folded over, but soon they'll stick up in typical Chihuahua fashion.

Chihuahuas have good senses of sight and hearing and make fine watchdogs. Because they're very fond of human company, they also make great companions. They can be jealous of their owners, so they need proper socialization. Their small size also requires gentle handling.

The Chihuahua does not need a lot of exercise. Running around the house or apartment will provide much of the exercise it needs. It is an indoor dog that likes warm temperatures. It does enjoy little outings in nice weather and likes a coat when it is chilly. Grooming is fairly simple. The long-coated Chi needs to be brushed a few times a week, while the smooth-coated variety can be wiped down with a damp cloth.

Like most puppies, chihuahuas should be groomed from four weeks of age. Have the little Chihuahua lie in your lap and relax for brushing and nail clipping.

There are many ideas about where Chihuahuas come from. Some people think that Chihuahua-like dogs were a part of ancient Mexican civilizations such as the Mayans, the Toltecs or the Aztecs. Others think the breed originated in Egypt or China. Some researchers believe that the breed was in Europe before the discovery of the New World, with certain paintings as evidence of this. Whatever the truth may be, the Chihuahua has long been associated with Mexico and is named for one of its northern states. The little dogs were taken north to the United States around the mid-1800s. It's a long way from their warm homeland, but today Chihuahuas are very popular in Canada.

Did you know that chihuahua is pronounced chih-wa-wa?

Height: 15–23 centimetres
Weight: 0.9–2.7 kilograms

All About Puppies!

What are Dogs?

Just like us, dogs are mammals — animals that have hair (or fur) and feed their babies with milk. Dogs belong to a family called *canidae* that includes wolves, jackals, foxes, coyotes and hyenas. Recent studies have shown that dogs and wolves are the same species, called *Canis lupus.* Dogs are really domesticated wolves. It was once thought that modern dogs probably had ancestors from more than one kind of wolf. But more recent studies show that dogs originated in East Asia from just a few domesticated wolves. As people migrated to other parts of the world, including North America, they took their dogs with them. Eventually, there were dogs in many places.

People and Dogs

The change from wolf to dog probably happened before people formed communities and started to grow crops. Wolves began to hang around human encampments for a share of the food and grew more domesticated. They became humans' hunting partners, thanks to their swiftness and their senses, which are many times keener than ours. Dogs also grew to be very good at reading human body language. They can pick up clues that other intelligent animals, including wolves and even primates, cannot.

Over time our canine friends moulded themselves into excellent human companions and workmates. They became smaller and more sociable. People began to develop different breeds by breeding dogs with traits that would be useful, attractive,

or otherwise desirable. Images of man's best friend show up in ancient paintings, drawings, pottery, porcelain, carvings and tapestries, and this art has helped scientists to figure out how different breeds came to be.

Breeds and Mixes

Because of the way that humans have bred them, dogs display more sizes and forms than any other species in the world. Many canine companions have been custom-made, because breeders chose the traits they wanted the next generation to have. This works because both dog parents pass on some of their traits to their pups.

Sometimes people set out to develop a new breed. The Labradoodle, for example, was bred in Australia as a non-shedding assistance dog, beginning in the 1970s. Originally consisting of a Poodle/Labrador Retriever mix (the North American version still does), the Aussie

Labradoodle now boasts relatives from six different breeds, including other retrievers and spaniels.

Genetic Diseases

Genetic diseases are ones that are passed down from parents to offspring through their genes. Purebred dogs tend to have more genetic problems than cross-bred dogs. Mixed-breed dogs, on average, live longer than purebreds. Good breeders try to get rid of genetic diseases by breeding only those dogs that have been tested and found to be free of disease. However, not all of these diseases have tests, and not all diseases that are carried show in the parents. Even dogs with two purebred parents of different breeds still have a high chance of having genetic problems. Some of the genetic diseases that are found in purebred dogs include hip and elbow dysplasia and other joint problems, epilepsy, eye conditions, skin conditions, collapsing windpipe and kidney problems.

Although many people prefer purebred dogs, many others believe that mixed-breed dogs also make great pets.

Dog Shows

Dog clubs in many countries, such as the American Kennel Club, the United Kennel Club, the Canadian Kennel Club, the Australian National Kennel Council and the Kennel Club UK, decide upon the desirable traits for a breed of dog. They write a description of the ideal dog of a breed, including its appearance and its temperament, called the breed standard. Standards may vary between the clubs. Judges use the standards at dog shows to determine which dogs are the best examples of their breeds. Undesirable characteristics are called faults and count against a dog. The dogs that win prizes at dog shows are much sought after as parents for new litters.

Dogs with Jobs

A dog's sense of smell is thought to be at least 10,000 times better than a human's. Because of that, dogs are very useful at sniffing out bombs and controlled substances. They can also find lost people, even those buried in snow or earth or wreckage. Some studies have shown that dogs might actually be able to smell changes that happen in the human body when a disease is present. Some dogs can even sense an epileptic seizure about to happen.

Dogs have also been bred to be helpful in other ways. Water dogs, such as the Newfoundland, have a strong instinct to pull people from water. We all know how well herding dogs round up livestock, and you've probably seen guide dogs leading the blind. There are also personal assistant dogs that help with all kinds of tasks, such as retrieving needed items, pulling wheelchairs and alerting the deaf to sounds. Border Collies, along with their handlers, are used to clear birds and other wildlife from airport landing strips. Clearly dogs are more than our best friends; they're also great helpers.

Stages of Puppy Development

Puppies are very immature when they are born, but develop quickly. Here are some of the key stages of puppy development.

Birth
    A puppy is born unable to see or hear, though it can feel, smell, cry and suck. It is totally dependent on its mother to feed it and keep it warm.

10 Days
    The pup's ears open.
12 Days
    Its eyes open.
3 Weeks
    This is a time of change as the pup develops its senses. It begins to crawl around and explore.
4-6 Weeks
    The pup learns how to be a dog. It tussles with littermates in play fights. Around the fifth week, the pup is also beginning to be weaned, and it starts to eat some solid foods.
7 Weeks
    It is important not to take the pup from its litter before this point, because it is still learning to socialize with other dogs.
8-9 Weeks
    At this age, the pup is easily frightened, so it should be treated with care. Early experiences are very important.

A Dog in the Home

Having a dog in the home is in many ways like having another person. A dog has needs and wants. It will need and want to be loved and cared for, to be fed well and exercised, to be taken for medical care when needed and to be protected from harm. Having a dog means extra work and expense, but also extra companionship.

If you decide to get a dog, there are several places you can go. There are many dog shelters and rescue facilities with wonderful dogs waiting to be adopted. There are breeders who choose dog parents carefully so that they can produce the healthiest puppies possible. There are also breeders who are not so careful, so ask a lot of questions of any breeder you might consider, especially about health and temperament. It is good to talk to people who have adopted dogs from the breeder. It is also a good idea to see where the pups are living and meet their mother. You should think carefully about what would be best for you and for the dog you might bring into your home. Learning more about dogs will help you make a wise choice.

A new dog in the home, whether a pup or an older adopted dog, needs

kindness and some quiet time to adjust to the new surroundings. Some dogs like a bed and a crate to call their own private area. Frequent trips outside for bathroom breaks help a new dog learn the routine and avoid mistakes. A chew toy gives a dog a satisfying quiet activity to relax with when its people are too busy to play.

The Dog Owner's Friends

Veterinarians can give dog owners good advice on how to take the best care of their dog. Vets give the proper inoculations and check for all kinds of ailments. They also help the dog get better if it's ill.

Some people like to take a training class with their dogs to help them learn to be good doggy citizens and owners. Many good books give detailed advice on how to train a dog. A companion dog will be happier if it can learn how to get along with people and other animals. Someone planning to get a dog has lots of homework to do. It's a big commitment.

Did You Know?

1. Dogs have no shoulder joints. Their front legs are attached to their bodies by muscle and sinew.

2. Before humans ever ventured into space, they sent up a dog named Laika, in Sputnik II, in 1957. Laika is the Russian word for barker and also the name of a breed of dog, the East Siberian Laika.

3. Dogs' eyes sometimes move under their lids when they are sleeping. Researchers think that this Rapid Eye Movement (REM) is like what people have, and it means that a dog is dreaming.

4. Just like children, puppies get a first set of teeth, which they lose, and then get their permanent teeth. If the baby teeth do not drop out in time, they might have to be removed.

5. Why are puppies so cute? It's because they're babies. Nature makes babies irresistible so parents and other adults will like them and care for them. Babies have big heads and big eyes. Their bodies catch up as they grow.

6. Dogs don't see as many colours as humans do, but they are much better at seeing movement. They can also see better in dim light. The placement of the eyes on a dog's head determines how much binocular (3D) vision a dog will have. Eyes on the front of the face give more binocular vision and to the side, less.